Terrible Tim!

Terrible Tim!

KATIE HAWORTH

LAURA HUGHES

templar publishing

Terrible Tim likes to

Terrible Tim likes to R O R

Terrible Tim
likes to dash...

Terrible Tim
likes to

SPLAS

DRAW

ROAR

DASH

SPLASH! Terrible,
terrible
Tim!

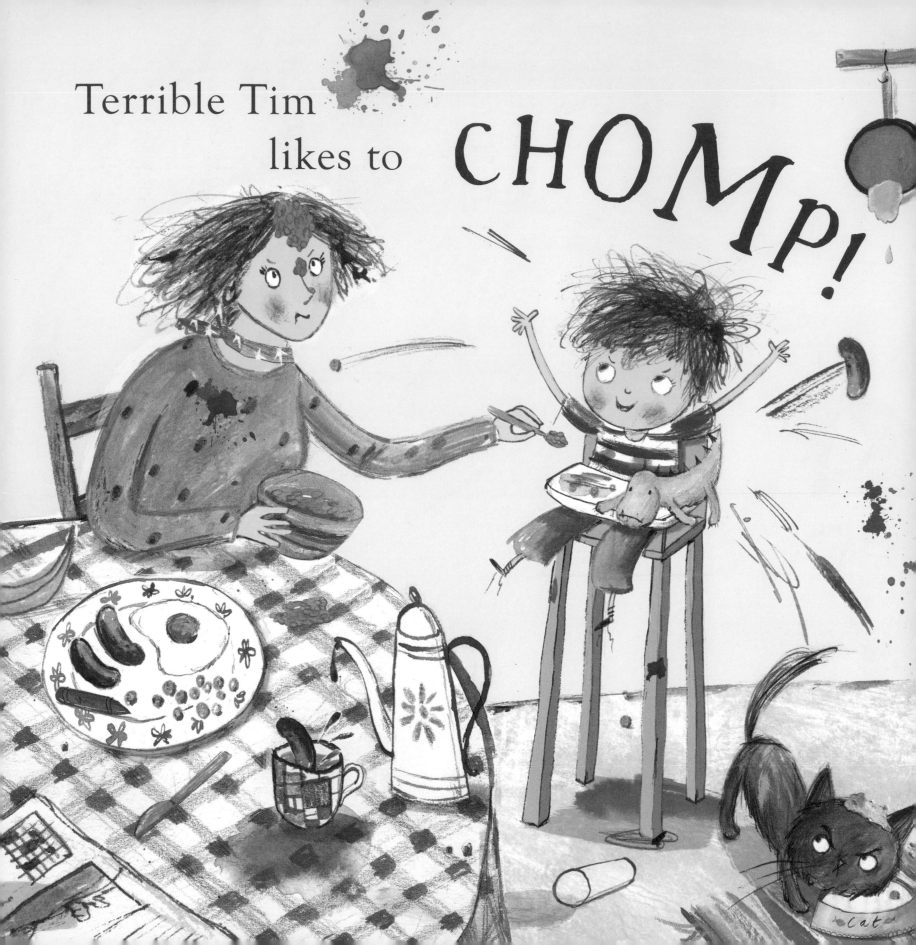

Terrible Tim
likes to

CHOMP!

Terrible Tim likes to

STOMP

Terrible Tim
likes to

Terrible Tim
likes to

CHOMP

STOMP

Terrible Tim
LIKES to

cuddle

Terrible Tim
LOVES to

snuggle

Night, night,
sleep tight,

Terrible,

TERRIBLE

Tim!

For Timmi who isn't
terrible at all, and who
built MW with
his bare hands

L.H.

For Archie, who
was the original
Tim, and for Thea,
who will be the
second if her mad
aunt has anything
to do with it

K.H.

A TEMPLAR BOOK

First published in the UK in 2016 by
Templar Publishing, part of the
Bonnier Publishing Group,
The Plaza, 535 King's Road, London,
SW10 0SZ www.templarco.co.uk
www.bonnierpublishing.com

Illustration copyright ©
2016 by Laura Hughes
Text and design copyright © 2016
by The Templar Company Limited

1 3 5 7 9 10 8 6 4 2

ISBN 978-1-78370-379-1 (Hardback)
ISBN 978-1-78370-502-3 (Paperback)

Designed by Verity Clark
Written by Katie Haworth
Edited by Alison Ritchie

Printed in China